This book belongs to

. . . .

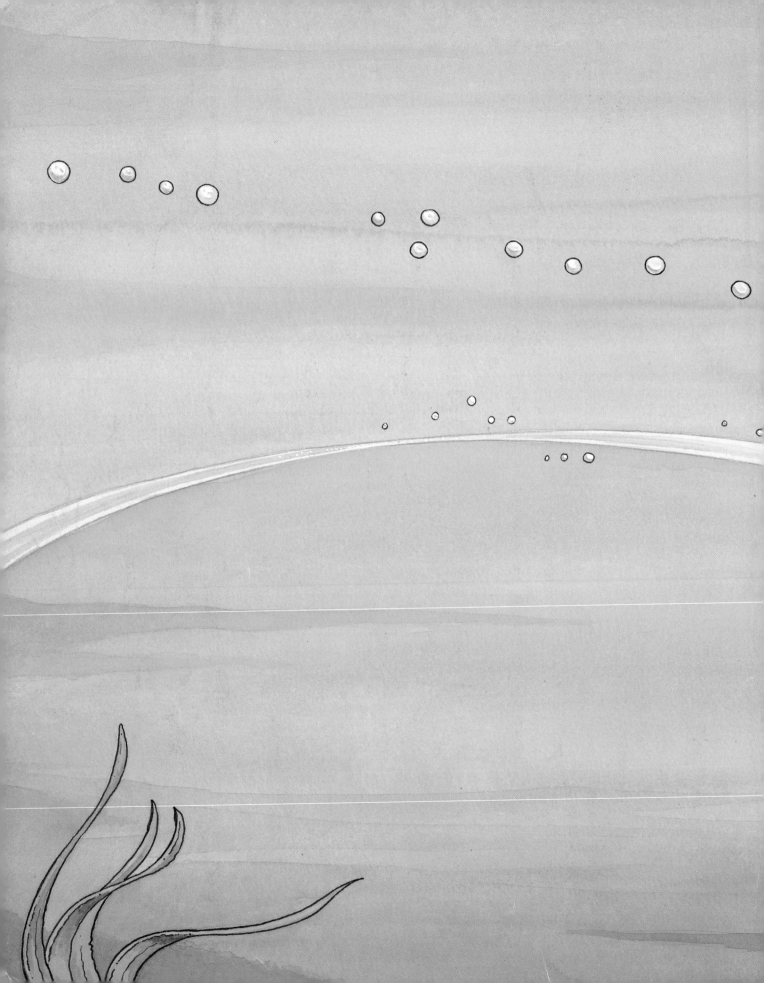

DON'T EAT THE BABYSITTER
A PICTURE CORGI BOOK 0 552 55115 5

First published in Great Britain by Picture Corgi,
an imprint of Random House Children's Books

This edition published 2005

1 3 5 7 9 10 8 6 4 2

Picture Corgi Books are published by Random House Children's Books,
61–63 Uxbridge Road, London W5 5SA,
a division of The Random House Group Ltd,
in Australia by Random House Australia (Pty) Ltd,
20 Alfred Street, Milsons Point, Sydney, NSW 2061, Australia,
in New Zealand by Random House New Zealand Ltd,
18 Poland Road, Glenfield, Auckland 10, New Zealand,
and in South Africa by Random House (Pty) Ltd,
Endulini, 5A Jubilee Road, Parktown 2193, South Africa

THE RANDOM HOUSE GROUP Limited Reg. No. 954009
www.kidsatrandomhouse.co.uk

A CIP catalogue record for this book is available from the British Library.

Printed in China

Don't Eat the Babysitter!

Nick Ward

Picture Corgi

*For Eileen and Tony
and babysitters everywhere*

Sammy and Sophie Shark were very excited! Mum and Dad had gone out for the evening and Anna, their favourite babysitter, had come to look after them.

But when Sammy became too excited,
he had the unfortunate habit (as all
young sharks do) of biting things!

"Supper's ready," called Anna.
"What is it?" asked Sammy,
rushing into the room.
"It's your favourite," said Sophie.
"Kiddie Fingers!"

"Yummy!" cheered Sammy.

He opened his mouth and...

"Oh Sammy," cried Sophie.
"Don't eat the supper tray!"
"Sorry," said Sammy.
"Never mind," said Anna.
"Let's play a game of cards."

"Brilliant," cried Sammy.
"Er...what do we do?"
"We turn the cards over," explained Anna,
"and if two cards match, the first one
to shout SNAP! wins."

They started to turn over their cards. First Anna, then Sophie, and then Sammy. His tail twitched with excitement.

"SNAP!" shouted Sophie when she saw two cards the same. "I won!"
"That's not fair," said Sammy.

"Never mind, Sammy,"
said Anna. "Let's play again."
Anna turned over another card.
Then Sammy went...

"Oh Sammy!" said Sophie. "It's SNAP not CRUNCH!"

"Sorry," blushed Sammy. "I didn't mean to."

"Never mind," said Anna, checking her watch. "Your favourite TV programme is just about to start."

Anna turned on the television.
"Terrors of the Deep!" said the announcer.

"Brilliant!" shouted Sammy,
and they settled down to watch.
Sammy's tail twitched with excitement.

"Deep in the inky black ocean," said the television, "lives the awesome giant octopus. He's huge and he's fierce and yum, yum, yum, he eats little sharks for breakfast!"

"Oh, NO!"
shouted Sammy.
He opened his mouth and...

"Oh Sammy," gasped Sophie.
"Don't eat the television!"
"Sorry," gulped Sammy. "It was
an accident."
"Never mind," smiled Anna.
"It's time for your bath now."

Sammy and Sophie loved bath time.
Sophie spread some bubbles on top
of a big yellow sponge.

"Who wants a piece of my
lovely sponge cake?" she asked.
"Me," cried Sammy, all in a lather.

He opened his mouth and...

CRUNCH!

"Oh Sammy," sighed Sophie.
"Don't eat the bath!"
"Sorry," spluttered Sammy.
"Never mind dear," said Anna.
"I think it's time for bed now."

"But I'm not tired," yawned Sammy
as Anna kissed him goodnight.
"I'm not tired," he mumbled as she
turned off the light.
"Just think of nice things," said Anna.
"You'll soon drift off to sleep."
"I'm not..." and Sammy fell fast asleep!

Sammy dreamt of his favourite things.
He dreamt of a big squashy
marshmallow, and...

CRUNCH!

went his pillow.

He dreamt of a big bar of
chocolate, and...

CRUNCH!

went his cupboard.

He dreamt of a big juicy burger, and...

CRUNCH!

went his bed.

"Wake up, Sammy," called Sophie. "You're eating the bedroom!"

"What's all this noise?" asked Anna the babysitter, diving into the room. Sammy was dreaming of a giant Kiddie Finger!

He opened his mouth and...

"SAMMY!" cried Sophie.

"DON'T EAT THE..."

Just then, Mum and Dad arrived home,
and Sammy woke up.
"Hello darlings," said Mum. "Have you
been good?"
"Well!" giggled Sophie. "Sammy ate the
TV and the supper tray, and the cards,
and the bath, and the bedroom and..."

"Where's Anna?" asked Mum.
"Yes, where's Anna?" said Dad.
"Oh Sammy," they cried,
"you didn't eat the..."

"No, here I am!" laughed Anna, "and they've both been very good little sharks ...
Haven't you, Sammy?"

But for once, Sammy kept his mouth firmly

SHUT!

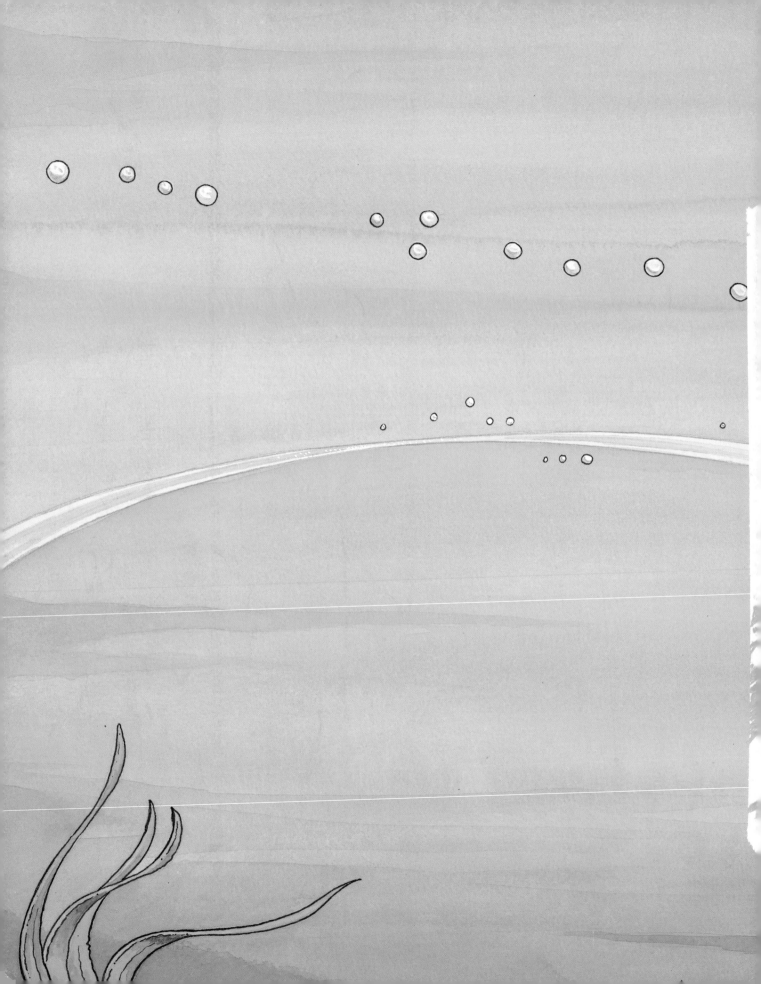

If you liked this,
you'll love . . .

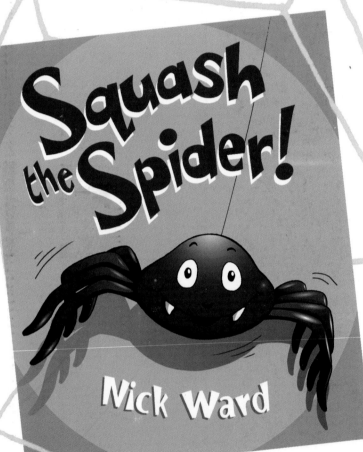